THE RAINMAKER

by Barbara Todd

art by Rogé

Annick Press

Toronto

New York

Vancouver

Clarence wondered.

He wondered how big the wind could be. "If it got really windy," thought Clarence, "maybe I could fly." He held a finger up to test the wind.

Nothing. But he liked to be prepared, so he did up the buttons on his coat.

He wondered if clouds tasted good.
If you ate one, would you float? He
wondered if he'd ever find the perfect
puddle. He wore boots just in case.
Clarence was ready for anything.

One day Clarence was so busy wondering, he nearly walked past the tap. He wouldn't have noticed it at all if it hadn't been for the sign that said "RAIN." (It used to say "DRAIN," but the "D" had worn off.)

"I wonder . . ." said Clarence. "If I turn on the tap, will I really make rain?"

He looked to see if anyone was watching, then he tried to turn the tap. It wouldn't turn at all.

Clarence used both hands and twisted as hard as he could.

Nothing came out.

"Where's the rain?"

PLOP! A drop fell on his head.

After the first drop came another. And another. It drizzled. It showered. Clarence could barely see across the street.

"Wow! It works!"

While Clarence splashed in puddles, a man stopped beside the tap.

"That's some rain you made. I see you found the tap."

"Is that your tap?" asked Clarence.

"Yesirree," said the Rainmaker. "Been in the family for years. Works like a charm, doesn't it? 'Course, some folks don't like getting wet. So if you're making rain, you've got to keep umbrellas handy."

By now a long line of people stood in front of the wheelbarrow.

"Will you please hurry up!" snapped the first woman. "This coat cost a fortune. It's getting wet!"

She opened an umbrella and a very strange thing happened: it stopped raining all around her. It only rained underneath the umbrella.

"Ridiculous!" she sputtered. She closed the umbrella and squelched down the street.

The next umbrella had a duck's head on the handle. An old man opened it and the duck went "QUACK!"

"Yikes!" cried the man. He dashed down the street, leaping over puddles as he went.

Clarence looked to see who was next. There was no one left. They'd all gone home.

"Would you like an umbrella?" asked the Rainmaker.
"Yes, please!" said Clarence.
"Try this one," he said. "It's my Windsailer Umbrella."
Clarence opened it and a gust of wind swirled out, pushing him along the street. It would have been perfect except he was flying upside down and backwards.

"It's not quite ready yet," admitted the
Rainmaker. "But that's enough for today. Here's
an umbrella for you. I think you'll like it.
With all this rain, it might come in handy."

He pushed his wheelbarrow slowly down the street. "Wait!" called Clarence. "How do I stop the rain?" "Turn off the tap!" The Rainmaker waved and disappeared around the corner.

Clarence splashed
over to the tap. He tried
to turn it off. It wouldn't
budge.

"Now what?"
Clarence wondered.
He hurried to the corner, but the Rainmaker
was gone. "I'd better go home."

Clarence opened his umbrella. It had a
propeller on one end.

"I wonder . . ." He gave the propeller a spin.
Clarence lifted off the ground and floated
down the street.

When he got home, Clarence had an idea.
He opened the phone book and looked under
"RAIN."

"Let's see," considered Clarence. "RAIN
BARRELS . . . RAIN BOOTS . . . RAINCOATS
. . . REINDEER . . . but no RAINMAKER."

The next morning it rained harder than ever.
Clarence grabbed his umbrella and went outside.
Water splashed up past his ankles.

"I need a boat!" said Clarence. "I wonder . . ."

He spun the propeller and sailed all the way to the tap.

There was the Rainmaker.

"Ahoy! Getting a bit damp, don't you think?"

"I couldn't turn off the tap," called Clarence.

"I noticed," replied the Rainmaker. "Try this." He handed Clarence an oil can.

Clarence squeezed a few drops onto the tap and tried again. "It works!"

The rain slowed to a sprinkle. Soon it was just a fine mist. One last drop fell. PLOP!

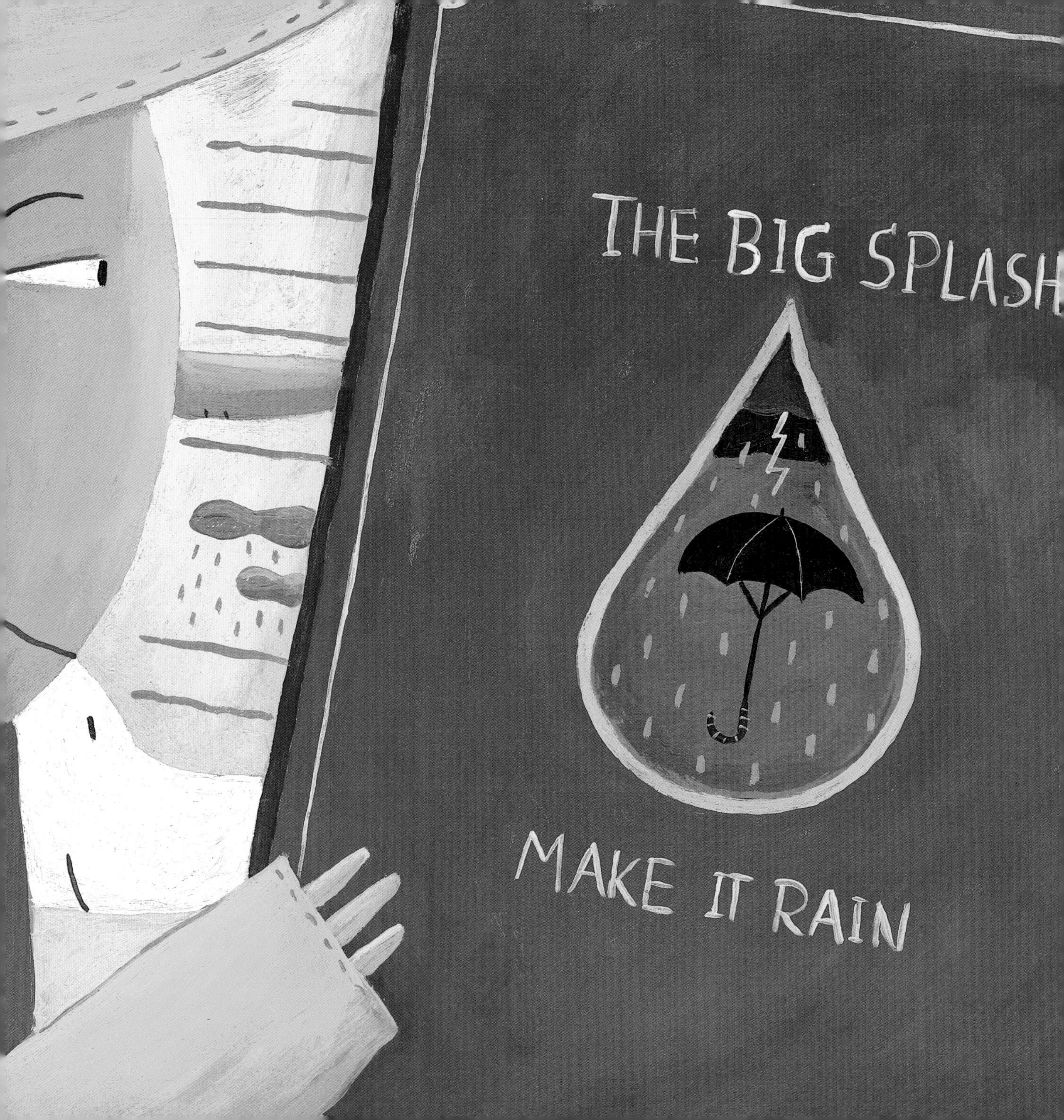
THE BIG SPLASH
MAKE IT RAIN

"You're a natural, kid! Not everyone can make rain, you know. I wonder . . . " said the Rainmaker. "How'd you like to help me out around here?"

"Wow! Really?"

"Sure," said the Rainmaker. "Just turn on the tap once in a while." He reached into the wheelbarrow. "You'd better take some umbrellas. And you'll need this."

He handed Clarence a book called THE BIG SPLASH: MAKE IT RAIN.

"It's all in there. Up to you what kind of rain you make. My favorite is Cats and Dogs. Hats and Frogs is fun too. But when it comes down in Buckets, watch out!"

He took a paint can and a brush out of the wheelbarrow. "This is for the Rainbows."

The Rainmaker gave Clarence a key. "What's this for?" asked Clarence.

"Thunder and Lightning," answered the Rainmaker. "I keep them locked up."

He shook Clarence's hand. "You'll do fine."
"See you," said Clarence.
On the way home Clarence wondered about things.
He wondered if a rainbow would fit in his backyard.
He wondered what made thunder grumble.

He was so busy wondering, he bumped into the mailman.
"Morning!" said the mailman. "Nice day after all, isn't it?"
Clarence looked up. There wasn't a cloud in the sky.
"You never know," said Clarence. "It just might rain."

© 2003 Barbara Todd (text)
© 2003 Rogé (illustrations)
Design: Sheryl Shapiro

We acknowledge the support of the Canada Council for the Arts, the Ontario Arts Council, and the Government of Canada through the Book Publishing Industry Development Program (BPIDP) for our publishing activities.

Cataloguing in Publication

Todd, Barbara, 1961-
    The rainmaker / by Barbara Todd ; art by Rogé.

ISBN 1-55037-775-2 (bound).—ISBN 1-55037-774-4 (pbk.)

I. Rogé, 1972- II. Title.

PS8589.O59R33 2003   jC813'.6   C2002-904324-7
PZ7

For Mom and Dad
—B.T.

A Lulu, Le petit chien du voisin qui a inspiré mon pinceau !
To Lulu, the neighborhood beagle who inspired my brush!
—R.G.

The art in this book was rendered in acrylic.
The text was typeset in Wade.

Distributed in Canada by:
Firefly Books Ltd.
3680 Victoria Park Ave.
Willowdale, ON
M2H 3K1

Published in the U.S.A. by Annick Press (U.S.) Ltd.
Distributed in the U.S.A. by:
Firefly Books (U.S.) Inc.
P.O. Box 1338
Ellicott Station
Buffalo, NY 14205

Printed in Canada by Friesens, Altona, Manitoba

Visit us at: www.annickpress.com